Rose and Rabbit
Celebrate Christmas

WANDA HOWELL
Illustrated by Dillon Olney & Christine Olney

For Caitlin Kreider

Our granddaughter, who suggested the items used for decorating the tree, especially, using the hubcap for the star at the top.

Out on the farm in the fresh white snow,
Rose and Rabbit were trying to decide where to go.

Should they watch farmer's wife make
presents look pretty?
Or should they take the sled and go into the city?

After talking it over they decided not to roam.
There was plenty to do right here at home.

"Farmer's wife is baking," said Rose,
"And it sure smells good.

I'd like to have a bite if only I could."

" Sweets aren't something we should eat
but it doesn't hurt to look.

We could modify the recipe
if we were allowed to cook."

"Have you noticed all of the holiday decorations?
Christmas is a really BIG celebration!

Candles in the window just seem to glow.
I think they are smiling at the snow below."

" Lots of houses have strings of lights.
They twinkle in the dark and make a pretty sight.

Almost every house has a Christmas tree.
Do you think we could decorate one for you and me?"

"There's a little pine tree out by the shed.
I think we can reach it if we stand on the sled.

Let's gather up some decorations
that are shiny and bright.
That will make our little tree look just about right."

"These old tin cans should do the job.

They will even sound pretty
when the wind makes them bob."

" And, Rose, they will sparkle just fine when the moon and
stars come out to shine."

"So, do you think we should put something on top?
That would really make our decorations pop!"

They finished their work and decided to rest.
Their little tree looked the absolute best.

Neighbors stopped by to sing Christmas carols that night.
A carol is music about Christmas, and it sounded just right.

Rose and Rabbit enjoyed the songs, so they
decided to sing along.
A feeling of joy and peace was there.
They could just feel it in the air.

Farmer said his family was coming today.
It's their holiday visit and they plan to stay.

That's why his wife has been so busy baking.
It's the reason for all the food she has been making.

Next day the farmer's family enjoyed a fine festive meal.

Then they planned to go into town
to hear the church bells peel.

There would be a live nativity on the church grounds.
That meant real live animals would be standing around.

Rose and Rabbit wanted to take part.
So they jumped in the truck before it could depart.

They stood by the manger with the cows
and the sheep.

They were silent; they didn't make a peep.

Farmer said, "This is a beautiful season because everything is done for a SPECIAL reason."

" Long, long ago something happened in a shed.
A baby was born with only hay for a bed.
That baby was Jesus and we celebrate His birth.
He was the sweetest baby ever born on this earth."

Suddenly, Rose thought she saw something in the sky.
It appeared that horses had learned how to fly.

It looked like horses were pulling the cart.
It seemed to be so full that it might come apart!

"Oh my!" said Rabbit, "That is good old Saint Nick. He has gifts for everyone and is lively and quick."

"Gifts for everyone? What a nice surprise! I hope what he brings me will be the right size."

"Everything about Christmas is just right," said Rabbit.
"Celebrating like this is a wonderful habit."

MERRY CHRISTMAS TO ALL
It's a very good night!

Wanda Howell was a wife, mother and grandmother. She was a fabric artist who designed and pieced beautiful quilts. This is the fourth and final book about the adventures of her imaginary characters, Rose and Rabbit, who lived on a real farm in Indiana. These books have been a tribute to her love of reading and writing stories for children.

After five years of lymphoma cancer treatments, Wanda died April 4, 2015.

Dillon Olney is a husband to his wonderful wife Sarah, who helped him finish this most special of Rose and Rabbit books. Dillon was honored to complete this series of books for Wanda and hopes you enjoy the prose and artwork as much as the creators enjoyed bringing these books to life!

Christine Olney grew up in a home where owning books and reading books were important. Later, she and her husband Jim carried on this tradition with their children. She is grateful to these people in her life who continue to support her love of children's literature and their encouragement of her artwork.

Made in the USA
San Bernardino, CA
23 October 2018